ONLY YOU

FILL EVERY DAY OF YOUR CHILD'S YEAR

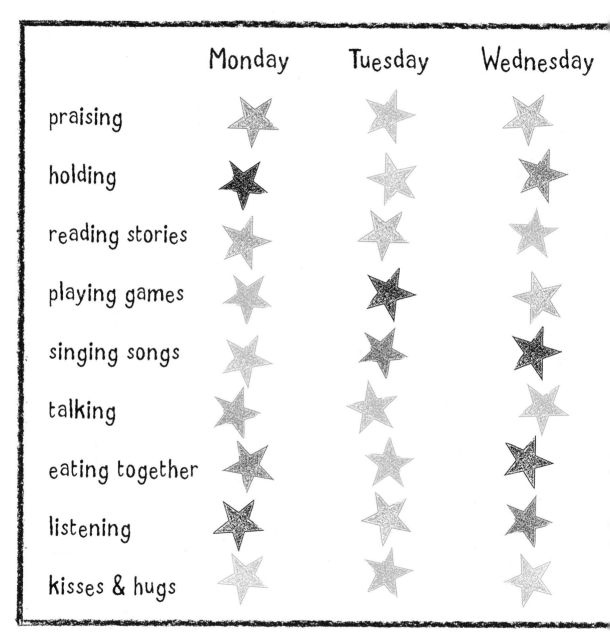

	Monday	Tuesday	Wednesday
praising	★	★	★
holding	★	★	★
reading stories	★	★	★
playing games	★	★	★
singing songs	★	★	★
talking	★	★	★
eating together	★	★	★
listening	★	★	★
kisses & hugs	★	★	★

WITH LOTS OF TIME TOGETHER!

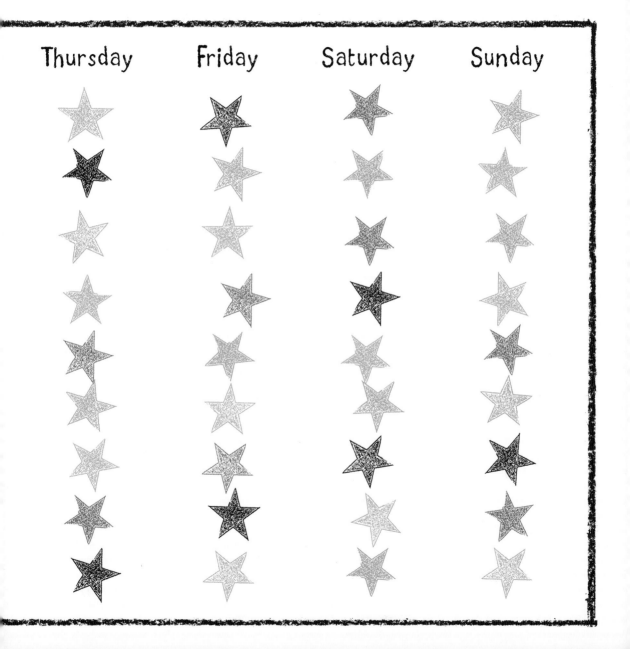

| Thursday | Friday | Saturday | Sunday |

ONLY YOU

ROSEMARY WELLS

VIKING

TIPS FOR READING TO TODDLERS

Here are some ways to get the most out of reading *Only You* and other books, with your toddler:

◆ When you read together, cuddle up with your child on your lap. Remember to look at each other as well as the book.

◆ Let your child lead. If your child wants to skip pages or read the same story again and again, it's okay.

◆ Ask your child to point out things in the pictures. For instance, ask, "Where is the balloon?" and have your child find it on the page.

◆ Ask your child to name things in the pictures and talk about them. Point to the train and ask, "What is this?" Then ask, "What sound does a train make?"

◆ Use the pictures to teach new words. Say, "See the trumpet? A trumpet is a loud instrument that makes music." Then pretend to play the trumpet.

◆ Use the story to start a conversation. Say, "It looks like the bears are baking. Remember when we baked cookies? What did we use to make them?"

◆ Ask questions about the story. "What are the bears doing in this picture?" Pause and then help your child answer. Allow your child to make things up.

◆ Act out parts of the story. If it says "you laugh and pick it up," then laugh out loud.

Here are some ways you can extend your toddler's learning "on the go":

1. Bring books to read while you wait in line at the market or at the doctor's office.

2. Talk about books you've read when you are at the park or on a walk. "Look! That lady is wearing a hat like the bear in the story we read."

3. Use a word or phrase from the story throughout the day. As you buckle your child into the car seat say, "Only you can make me giggle when you smile."

bornlearning℠

CIVITAS | United Way SUCCESS BY 6 | United Way

For Rachel Hodges

VIKING
Published by the Penguin Group
Penguin Putnam Books for Young Readers,
345 Hudson Street, New York, New York 10014, U.S.A.

Penguin Books Ltd, Registered Offices: Harmondsworth, Middlesex, England

First published in 2003 by Viking,
a division of Penguin Putnam Books for Young Readers.

3   5   7   9   10   8   6   4   2

LIBRARY OF CONGRESS CATALOGING-IN-PUBLICATION DATA:
Wells, Rosemary.
Only you / by Rosemary Wells.
p. cm.
Summary: A little bear describes how much his mother means to him.
ISBN 0-670-03634-X
Special Markets ISBN 978-0-670-06289-8
Not for Resale
[1. Mother and child—Fiction. 2. Bears—Fiction.] I. Title.
PZ7.W46843 On 2003
[E]—dc21
2002015570

Manufactured in China
Set in Minister

This Imagination Library edition is published by Penguin Group (USA), a Pearson
company, exclusively for Dolly Parton's Imagination Library, a not-for-profit
program designed to inspire a love of reading and learning, sponsored in part by The
Dollywood Foundation. Penguin's trade editions of this work are available wherever
books are sold.

ONLY YOU

Only you can show me I can do
anything I try!

I'm the apple of your eye.
Only you.

Only you . . .
don't mind what I do.

Over goes your coffee cup,
but you laugh and pick it up.
Only you.

Only you . . .
can make my dreams come true.

Dreams lie sleeping in my heart,
waiting for my world to start.
Only you.

Only you . . .
can turn my gray sky blue.
Without you near,

I feel so very small.
How I wait to hear
your footsteps in the hall.

The only place I want to be
is in your lap or on your knee.

Only you.
Only me.

The first three years of a child's life are important in so many ways. Young children learn by living. Everything they see and do helps them understand the world and how it works. When parents spend time with their children, the children grow and glory in the special attention of the people they know and love best. In the games and rituals that develop around household chores, errands, mealtime, naps, playtime, and bedtime, children find security, comfort, and the courage to explore. From close relationships with their parents, young children learn what it is to be loved.

Children make remarkable developmental progress in the first three years of life—learning language, social skills, and physical coordination. They learn to play with other people and to understand that other people have needs and feelings. It's a joy to watch your child grow and develop. Parents can encourage this development—not by "teaching" their children lessons, not by buying them lavish educational equipment, but by giving them one-on-one time. This positive parental attention shows children, over and over, that they are loved. With this knowledge, children will build the basic security and confidence that they need to take on the world.

—*Dr. Perri Klass*

FILL EVERY DAY OF YOUR CHILD'S YEAR

	Monday	Tuesday	Wednesday
praising	★	★	★
holding	★	★	★
reading stories	★	★	★
playing games	★	★	★
singing songs	★	★	★
talking	★	★	★
eating together	★	★	★
listening	★	★	★
kisses & hugs	★	★	★

WITH LOTS OF TIME TOGETHER!

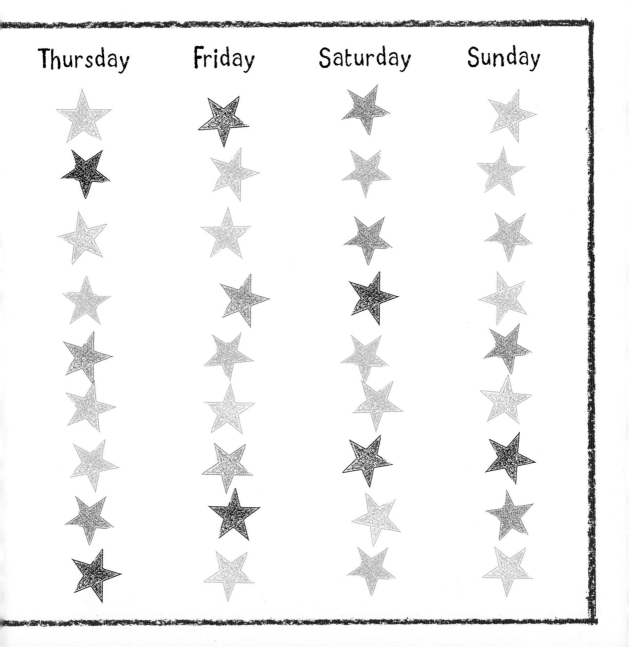